Peter Silverman found out about paranormals the prior year when one of his best friends—Waylon—bonded with a sea-horse shifter. For the most part, he doesn't think much of the fact that other beings exist right alongside humans as it doesn't affect his job as a paramedic. That all changes when he begins running across injured people with holes in their necks. To Peter, they look suspiciously like a vampire's bite.

Bringing his suspicions to Waylon's shifter lover, Peter is introduced to Pisces, who's supposed to be one of the shifter pod's best trackers. The bottlenose dolphin shifter immediately claims that Peter is his mate. Peter knows that means he's supposed to be the other half of Pisces's soul, but he insists on a date.

The scent of a shifter on Peter has the unexpected repercussion of drawing the attention of the rogue vampire. Can Peter evade the rogue's clutches while accepting a reality that has changed yet again?

Sailing with a Dolphin
Copyright © 2023 Charlie Richards
ISBN: 978-1-4874-4083-1
Cover art by Angela Waters

Published by eXtasy Books Inc

Look for us online at:
www.eXtasybooks.com

Sailing with a Dolphin Beneath Aquatica's Waves: Book Sixteen 16

By

Charlie Richards

DEDICATION

*You will never 'find' time for anything. If you want time, you
must make it.*
~Charles Buxton

CHAPTER ONE

"Ma'am? Can you tell me your name?"

Peter Silverman stared into the glassy eyes of the woman lying on the pavement. He didn't think he would get a response to his question, but he had to try. It was part of his job, after all.

While his partner paramedic—Ryley Cauldwell—checked the woman's vitals, Peter tried to get the woman to focus and engage. They swapped roles depending on the situation. Having worked together for nearly six years—Peter had been paired with Ryley right out of training, with Ryley being an older and experienced paramedic—they had their system down and could often anticipate what the other person would do in any situation.

"Blood pressure is way too damn low," Ryley muttered, before shining a pen light in the woman's eyes. All she did was blink. "Pupil response nearly nonexistent."

Sweeping his gaze over the prone woman once more, Peter racked his brain for some sign of injury. He'd just focused on her face again when something snagged his attention. Curling the tips of his fingers around the top of her blouse at her shoulder, Peter carefully tugged it aside.

The sight of the twin holes in the flesh where her neck met her shoulder caused his stomach to churn.

"Ryley," Peter murmured, lifting his gaze to his partner. "We got another one."

"Shit," Ryley snarled, drawing the word out. "That's four in two weeks." Turning his attention to Peter, he shook his

1

head. "What the hell is going on, Petey?"

Even though Peter would prefer to be called his given name while working, he didn't correct Ryley. He'd been called that by his mother since before he could remember. His friends had picked it up, and it had trickled down from there into his work associates.

"I'll get the gurney," Peter declared, rising to his feet.

Peter hustled back to the ambulance. It wasn't as if he could explain to Ryley that he suspected a rogue vampire was haunting the streets of Sacramento. Over a year before, Peter had learned that the paranormal actually existed and lived and worked right alongside humans, hiding in plain sight. One of his best buddies—Waylon—had ended up bonding with a seahorse shifter named Colton, of all things.

Crazy shit.

As Peter rolled the gurney to Ryley's side where he still checked on the woman, an idea formed. If there really was a rogue vampire on the streets, then he should report it to Colton and the guy's leader.

Uh, alpha. Right. The leader of the marine life shifter pod is called an alpha.

Peter worked on auto-pilot as he helped Ryley get the breathing and apparently awake but unresponsive woman onto the gurney and into the ambulance. He set up an IV as Ryley closed the doors and rushed around to the front. He'd just finished attaching the O-negative blood bag to her port when he heard the driver's side door close.

"Ready?" Ryley asked.

"Yep," Peter responded while double-checking the straps holding the woman to the rolling bed. "You didn't see a purse or anything, did you?" he asked, suddenly realizing he'd forgotten to look around the alley where she'd been reported by some anonymous person.

"No, nothing but trash in that alley," Ryley grumbled as he started the ambulance moving. "As if they were dumping her with the other garbage." Letting out a low growl, Ryley snarled, "People can be such shitheads."

Peter scoffed. "Yeah."

*

Once Peter's shift was finished, he waved goodbye to a tired-looking Ryley and hurried home. He showered in record time before tugging on a pair of jean shorts and a polo shirt. After donning his sandals, Peter grabbed his keys, wallet, and shades and headed back out the door.

The kind of discussion he needed to have with Waylon and Colton needed to be done in person.

As Peter began driving north out of the city, he figured he should at least give Waylon a heads up that he was coming. He certainly didn't want to show up unannounced and interrupt something. Their mutual friend Jake had done that once, and the guys still razzed him about it.

Placing his phone in the holder on the dash, Peter hit a couple of buttons and attached it to the *Bluetooth* speaker in his newer model *Jeep Grand Cherokee*. The phone rang so many times that he feared he would need to leave a message. Just as he was sure voicemail would pick up, Peter heard a breathless Waylon answer.

"Hey, man. Give me just a sec."

Peter cringed, thinking maybe he'd interrupted something after all. Glancing at the time, he frowned. It was just after four in the afternoon. Peter and Ryley had been on the early shift for the last couple of weeks, although that was due to change.

"No prob, Way." Peter waited patiently as he drove toward *World of Aquatica*, the marine park owned and operated by shifters who could turn into a variety of marine life. Peter had learned that was the only reason the park could put on a tiger shark show. The tiger sharks used in the show were actually shifters, so they could think and reason even in their shark forms. Peter had seen the show a number of times, and he still found it fascinating.

"Sorry about that," Waylon told him, returning to the line. "I'm at the bar, and there was a rush, but I figured if you're calling me right after your shift, it's probably important." Waylon's deep voice took on a concerned note. "You usually spend at least half an hour in your sauna after your shift, considering it can be so physically demanding."

"You're right, but this is sort of important." Before Waylon could question him further, Peter told him, "And I'm not comfortable talking about it over the phone." Peter hesitated a second, then added, "And I was hoping to talk to both you and Colton."

"Oh," Waylon murmured, his voice going quiet. "It's like that, huh?"

"Yep." Peter figured his smart friend would get the reference. What he needed to talk to them about might have paranormal connotations. "I'm driving your way now." Considering Waylon said he was at the bar working—Waylon worked as a bartender at one of Aquatica's restaurants—Peter asked, "Do you get off any time soon?"

"I'm here until six," Waylon told him. "And Colton won't be available until probably thirty minutes after that. He's working in the aquarium until then."

Peter knew that meant Colton was in his seahorse form and actually *in* the aquarium. Most of the shifters there took turns in the aquariums to show visitors various marine life. Unless the shifter was something too exotic—such as the alpha and beta, who shared their psyche with huge squids—or a couple of security guards who turned into animals thought to be extinct.

"Okay." *Damn. Guess I shouldn't have rushed into this without thinking. I could've still had my sauna time.* "Well, I'll be at the park in twenty minutes, so I'll just wander the exhibits until you're off."

"You're welcome to come hang out at the bar with me," Waylon offered. "Are you hungry?"

"Yeah, okay," Peter agreed, even as his stomach growled at the mention of food. "I could certainly eat." With a laugh, he admitted, "I kinda rushed out the door without thinking after work."

Waylon hummed softly. "Sounds serious."

"Could be," Peter replied, sobering.

"I'll put in an order for the clam strip basket and fries for you in about ten minutes," Waylon told him, knowing exactly what Peter would want to eat. His buddy knew him well. "That way, it'll be hot and fresh when you get here."

"Thanks, man." Peter hummed as his mouth watered with anticipation. "I appreciate it."

"Sure. See you soon."

Waylon closed the call, and Peter pressed on the accelerator just a little bit harder. Noting his speed, he sighed and eased back off again. Getting pulled over for speeding wouldn't get him to the park any faster.

Peter arrived and headed to the VIP parking area near the front. After parking, he leaned over and opened the glove box. From within, he pulled the VIP tag that Colton had provided for all of Waylon's friends. After hanging it on his rearview mirror, Peter exited, locked his door, and headed toward the park.

Showing his annual pass to the attendant at the gate—also provided by Colton—Peter made his way into the park. As he headed toward the restaurant, he noticed the billboard with show times of the marine life shows. A stab of disappointment filled Peter when he saw he wouldn't be able to make the last tiger shark show if he sat down to eat. Then Peter grinned when he noticed that if he ate fast, he *would* be able to see the dolphin show.

That'll be a great distraction after I eat.

With that plan in mind, Peter hurried to the restaurant.

Pisces swam into the huge aquarium with Angelina by his side. Having worked with the fellow bottlenose dolphin on many occasions, he easily kept pace beside her. They'd done this routine so many times, he figured he could do it in his sleep.

Listening to Gerard introduce them as George and Gracy, Pisces prepared to do their first trick. The man had a mild Australian accent, which most found pleasing to the ear. After shows, while Pisces swam around so people could take pictures, he always got a kick out of how many people flirted with the man. Of course, these days, Gerard gently let people down, seeing as the weedy sea dragon shifter had met his mate.

A pang of jealousy stirred within Pisces, and he did his best to push it down. Over the years, a number of shifters in his pod had found their fated mate—the person who was the other half of their soul. Pisces always hoped the fates would smile upon him and he would meet his special someone soon.

The vibration of a stick tapping the water twice drew Pisces's attention. Knowing the cue, he undulated his powerful tail as he arched his body. Pisces leaped from the water, Angelina right beside him doing the same, and twirled in the air. Adjusting in mid-air, Pisces made certain to splash a large wave at the waiting crowd, soaking the first two rows.

Before being fully submerged again, Pisces took a deep breath through his blowhole. In that instant, the most tantalizing scent registered. Pisces enjoyed the smell so much that he nearly rose back to the surface to try to get another hint of it.

Pisces caught himself just in time and continued with the routine. That didn't stop him from searching for the scent each time he did a trick. Every time he used his tail to dance across the top of the water, Pisces searched for more.

When Barry — their *trainer* — was riding Pisces's back — one foot on him and the other on Angelina — he finally realized the delicious fragrance was coming from someone in the stands . . . and what it meant.

Holy shit! My mate is somewhere in block A, B, or C. How the hell will I be able to find him?

At that realization, Pisces's mind blanked a little. He pushed too hard through the water, breaking stride with Angelina. Barry was still on their backs and hissed his name, redrawing Pisces's focus. It was a good thing Barry was a harbor seal shifter with heightened reflexes, or he would have tumbled into the water.

Oops!

It took every scrap of self-control Pisces had to continue the routine. He knew he couldn't very well stop everything, shift, and go hunting for that special someone, even though every fiber of his being screamed at him to do just that. Instead, Pisces did his job.

Still, each time Pisces swam by the area where he knew his mate sat, he searched the stands — not that it helped. There was absolutely no way for him to pinpoint who the mouthwatering aroma belonged to.

As soon as the show was finished, Pisces couldn't help himself. Even as the people continued to mill around, snapping pictures of them, he swam to the far side of the aquarium. He rubbed his side against a tile that appeared like any other. It depressed ever-so-slightly.

In each aquarium and tank, there was a button. If, for some reason, a shifter had an emergency and needed to leave a shift early, the Roush brothers — their pods' alpha and beta — had planned for that contingency. Each place had a panel that a shifter could push with their snout, body, or even a fin. It would set off an alarm in the security office, and immediate action would be taken to have the shifter removed from the aquarium.

Pisces desperately needed that to happen . . . and fast.

To Pisces's relief, through the haze of the water, he saw several people arrive. The first was Eban, their head of security. The next was Gunner, a fellow bottlenose dolphin shifter. Gunner was usually paired with Sylvia for dolphin shows, and Pisces figured he was there to replace him. The final person making up the trio was Doctor Anthony.

Probably called because I asked to be removed.

As soon as the last of the visitors filed out, Eban closed the doors.

Pisces quickly shifted, taking on his human form. As soon as possible, he pulled himself from the pool. He took the towel Doc Anthony handed him and began drying himself, uncaring of his nudity.

"What happened, Pisces?" Barry asked, giving him a worried look. "You've never faltered before."

"Are you injured?" Doc Anthony asked, sweeping his gaze over his frame in an assessing manner. "Pull a muscle or something?"

"Is that why you asked to be removed?" Eban asked, resting his hands on his hips.

"I smelled my mate while in the air doing tricks," Pisces quickly explained, nodding at Gunner in thanks as the guy grinned and offered him congratulations before diving into the water. "He was sitting somewhere in areas A through C."

Scoffing, Barry grinned at him. "That would explain it."

Eban nodded. "Okay. I'll have Ovram start pulling footage. Maybe he can do a facial rec or something like that." He patted Pisces on the shoulder, offering him a grim smile. "We'll find your mate."

Relief filled Pisces as he nodded. "Thanks." Ovram was

their pod's technical guru. If anyone could help him start meeting the people in the stands, he could.

Before he could say more, Eban's phone rang. As the head enforcer answered the call, Pisces took the clothes the doc offered him and pulled them on. Then he slipped his feet into the sandals that Gunner had discarded before folding the other man's clothes.

"Glad you're out of the water already," Eban stated, drawing Pisces's attention as he lowered his phone. "Alpha Kaiser has a tracking job for you." Beckoning, Eban started toward the door. "Come on."

Pisces would much rather have stalked the park trying to find his mate, but he knew an order when he heard it. Following Eban, he hoped whatever his alpha needed wouldn't take long. Pisces followed Eban out the doors and settled onto the passenger seat of the utility cart the guy must have used to get there so swiftly.

Eban drove them out of the park to the attached private residential area. There were condos as well as a few homes scattered about the area. Stopping before the main complex that contained offices and conference rooms, Eban put the cart into *park*.

Without a word, Pisces followed the head enforcer through the building to Alpha Kaiser's large office.

As Pisces drew close to the door, the scent he was becoming obsessed with finding lingered in the air. His mouth watered, and his arousal spiked. Just as Eban opened the door, he paused and turned toward him, arching a brow in silent question.

Eban had obviously scented his arousal.

Pisces couldn't help it. He grinned as he moved past the enforcer. "You won't have to contact Ovram about the security footage," he declared as he looked around the room. His gaze fell on the only man that he didn't recognize—a black-haired male with worry filling his beautiful brown eyes.

"Why?" Eban closed the door behind them.

"Because that's my mate," Pisces murmured, unable to tear his gaze away from the gorgeous human before him.

CHAPTER TWO

That's my mate.

Peter felt his lips part as shock flooded him. "I-I am?" he would forever deny the squeak in his voice.

The handsome man's honey-brown eyebrows shot up as a rakish grin curved his full lips. "Yep." He slowly moved closer, as if he were stalking Peter. His hazel eyes turned predatory, and he licked his bottom lip. "You know what that means?"

Sucking in a sharp breath, Peter clenched his hands in his lap as the man drew close enough to touch. "Yeah."

"Glad you could join us, Pisces," Alpha Kaiser rumbled, drawing Peter's attention and interrupting his staring. Amusement laced his deep voice. "You arrived more swiftly than I'd anticipated, you being part of the dolphin show, after all."

"I was already out of the water, Alpha," Pisces admitted, settling on the other half of the small sofa. He brazenly rested his left arm across the back and leaned toward Peter. "Because I scented you at the show." Pisces reached out with his right hand and skimmed his forefinger along Peter's jaw, causing the hairs at his nape to stand on end. "And I needed to find you." He issued a soft scoff as his smile turned wry. "And here you are, and you know about us, don't you?"

Peter forced his voice to come out steady as he confirmed, "I know you're a shifter. Although I don't know what kind you are."

"Bottlenose dolphin." Pisces raked a heated gaze over Peter, causing his blood to heat in his veins, warming him from the inside out. "You were at the show. I damn near botched the whole show when I scented you."

Surprise filled Peter even as he fought the rush of desire he felt caused by Pisces's proximity. "Really? You were there, too?"

"Yep," Pisces confirmed. With a chuckle, he admitted, "Scenting our mate for the first time can be distracting as hell."

"Sorry," Peter murmured because it seemed like the right thing to do. "Didn't mean to."

"I'm not sorry," Pisces countered, even as he slid his hand up to cradle Peter's jaw and leaned toward him. "I'm fucking ecstatic."

Peter knew Pisces intended to kiss him. His intention was obvious. Feeling his pulse spike, Peter instinctively licked his bottom lip in anticipation.

Pisces groaned softly before settling his lips over Peter's. The warm press of his mouth against Peter's own drew a quiet whimper from him as his mind began to shut down. Peter felt Pisces gently nip his bottom lip, asking for entrance, and he couldn't resist opening.

When Pisces dipped his tongue into Peter's mouth, the shifter's flavor exploded across his taste buds—deep, rich, and masculine. Returning the kiss, he pressed forward, searching for more. Pisces didn't disappoint, sliding his hand to his nape so he could direct the kiss and deepen it.

All too soon, Peter heard not just a knock on the door, but the sound of a deep voice clearing his throat. The noises were better than a bucket of ice water. Peter yanked back, panting harshly as he stared in shock at the guy—shifter—who'd just about made his brain melt out of his ears.

Feeling a wealth of embarrassment flood him, Peter

glanced around furtively. He couldn't remember the last time he'd reacted to someone so viscerally. Peter had certainly never made out in front of anyone before. While he didn't consider himself a prude, he felt that such displays should be done in private.

As Peter swept his attention over everyone, he spotted various expressions. His buddy, Waylon, was relaxing back on the sofa he shared with his lover, Colton, and he was grinning broadly at him. Eban was leaning against the wall, his arms crossed, and he smirked at him.

Kaiser was probably the one who'd cleared his throat, but he wasn't looking at them. Instead, he was focused on the pair standing in the doorway. Peter recognized the huge dark-skinned male as Dare, another enforcer, glancing between Peter and Pisces with confusion in his eyes. The pale-blond with him appeared amused even as he arched one brow in silent question while focusing on Pisces.

Pisces lowered his left arm from the back of the sofa and tightened it around Peter's shoulders. Drawing him closer, he claimed, "He's my mate." Then he winked at Peter and asked, "So, what's your name, cutie?"

"P-Peter," he replied, still reeling from the undeniable pull he felt to the man next to him. "Peter Silverman."

"So nice to meet you, Peter," Pisces claimed, and Peter finally understood the expression *smoldering*. The heat in Pisces's eyes practically sent him up in flames. "I can't wait to get you alone so we can get to know each other better."

With the innuendo in Pisces's tone, Peter knew exactly what *getting to know each other better* would entail.

Feeling overwhelmed, Peter blurted, "I think we need to date first."

Pisces blinked once, twice, and the unmistakable look of disappointment flittered across his features — there and gone so fast that Peter would have missed it if he hadn't been star-ing right at him. Then Pisces smiled as he nodded once. "If that's what you need, Peter." He teased his fingertips along his opposite shoulder soothingly. "You're my mate, and I'll give you whatever time you need."

Peter felt a measure of relief mixed with disappointment, which confused him to no end.

Doing his best to dismiss it, Peter whispered, "Thanks." He tore his gaze away from Pisces and focused on Alpha Kaiser. After swallowing to get moisture into his suddenly too-dry throat, Peter stated, "So, uh, I guess I need to talk to you about vampires."

Vampires? Why does my mate need to talk about vampires?

That had been Pisces's first thought the prior day when he'd first met Peter. Listening as his mate explain what he and his partner had begun running into on the streets as paramed-ics, he'd felt a wealth of protective worry surge through him. Considering Peter requested a date before spending much time with him, Pisces had wasted no time in agreeing to hunt the streets for said rogue vampire.

While Peter's request completely sucked — *after all, he knows about paranormals and mates* — Pisces tried his best to seem un-derstanding. At least tracking had given him something to do that evening.

He's my mate. I'll give him the time he needs.

Pisces visited the four locations Peter had indicated where they'd picked up the bitten and traumatized victims. All three were inside alleyways around the corner from clubs. They weren't in seedy sections of town, but they were dimly lit ar-eas with parking lot lights that had been broken. There were also garbage bins and trash obscuring the scents.

Still, Pisces was able to pick up hints of the blood, dirt, body odor, and a dark iron-heavy scent that didn't have to do with the blood. In the last place Peter had picked up the woman, there was also the lingering scent of fear, which was understandable. The sickly-sweet tones of sadistic arousal had damn near turned Pisces's stomach.

Great. He's not just feeding. He's getting off on traumatizing his victims.

Pisces had hated sharing those findings with Alpha Kaiser. It meant he wouldn't stop on his own. Someone would have to find him and stop him.

Hopefully I'll just be able to find him, and I'll be able to pass on his location to Alpha Kaiser.

If Pisces didn't miss his guess, his alpha would prefer to share the information with Master Aldor Bercham. The vampire headed up a coven that resided south of Sacramento. Alpha Kaiser was on good terms with them, and they occasionally collaborated.

In truth, Pisces was a little surprised that his alpha hadn't already asked the vampires for assistance, but he supposed they needed proof that the problem was actually a rogue vampire first.

The sound of knocking on Pisces's door pulled him out of his thoughts. Grabbing the thin jacket he'd laid over the back of his sofa earlier, he headed to the door. Pisces opened it, not surprised to find Gunner standing there, a rakish grin on his features.

"Hey, I caught ya," Gunner rumbled, holding out a bouquet of roses. "Here."

Pisces stared at the flowers for a couple of seconds before meeting his friend's gaze. "Why are you trying to give me flowers?"

Gunner rolled his brown eyes while shaking his head. "So you can give them to Peter, ya dip shit," he told him, holding them out again. With a smirk, the fellow dolphin shifter claimed, "I know you wouldn't have thought of it. A romantic, you are not."

"And you are?" Pisces replied with a scoff. Still, he took the flowers from Gunner. They were a good idea. Except. "What if he doesn't like flowers? He's not a girl, ya know."

Shrugging, Gunner shoved his hands into his pockets as he took a step backward. "Everyone likes flowers, even if they don't admit it."

Pisces didn't know about that, but he figured it would be the thought that counted. "Well, thanks," he conceded, tossing his jacket over the crook of his arm that held the flowers. He lifted them in acknowledgment as he grabbed his wallet and shoved it into his back pocket. "It certainly can't hurt."

After swiping his keys, Pisces headed out of his apartment. "Sorry I had to pull you in yesterday. No way would I have been able to stay in the aquarium," he admitted as Gunner fell into step beside him and joined him in striding down the hall to the stairwell. Residing on the second floor, Pisces rarely bothered with the elevator.

"Hey, no worries, man." Gunner patted him on the shoulder. "I get it." With another ready grin, he held the stairwell door open for him. "And when it's my turn, I know that you'll do the same for me."

"Damn straight," Pisces responded agreeably.

Once on the ground floor, Pisces led the way out of the stairwell and across the lobby.

Gunner opened the front door and held it open, pausing there and patting him on the shoulder as he passed. "Good luck, man." With a wink, he added, "Go woo your man."

Pisces returned Gunner's grin. "I'm on it."

Then Pisces hurried to his *Jeep* and climbed behind the wheel. He placed the roses carefully on the floorboard of the passenger side before buckling himself in. His phone went into a cupholder, and he finally fired up his vehicle.

Once Pisces had exited the parking area and turned on the road, he pressed harder on the gas pedal. He reveled in the feel of the wind in his hair, blowing through the cab of his open-topped *Jeep*. Pisces knew the rainy season was coming, but for now, it was still warm enough and dry enough to cruise with the top down.

Pisces followed the GPS instructions, easily finding Peter's house. His mate had a home in an older, established neighborhood north of the city. He admired the large trees as well as the front porch with a porch swing. The two-story home wasn't huge or anything, but it certainly didn't scream bachelor pad, either, and Pisces wondered how his mate afforded it. It had an attached two-car garage, and he could see a shop farther back.

Parking in front of the garage, Pisces felt his anticipation ramp up. A skitter of nerves fired through him. He took a deep breath, then a second one, then grinned.

This is my mate, a gift from Fate. It'll work out.

After that mental pep-talk, Pisces grabbed the flowers and slipped out of the vehicle. He headed up the sidewalk to the porch and took the four steps two at a time. Once at the front door, Pisces blew out another breath and rang the bell.

Pisces strained his superior shifter hearing, searching for sounds from inside. At first, there was nothing. Shifting his weight from foot to foot, Pisces was contemplating hitting the bell again when he heard movement from within.

A few seconds later, the door opened, revealing his handsome mate smiling tentatively at him.

Once again, Pisces inhaled Peter's sweet, masculine aroma. His blood heated in his veins, and he barely kept from swaying. Pisces wanted to press against Peter and bury his face in the crook of his neck and just bask in his fresh scent.

"Hi, baby," Pisces managed roughly. "You smell amazing." He quickly cleared his throat and tried again. "Look amazing, too."

Peter did, too. He had on a pair of light-colored jeans that hugged his thighs and cradled his package just perfectly. His short-sleeved polo shirt molded to his torso, giving enticing peeks of his muscular body. Even the way his black hair was pulled away from his face accentuated his high cheekbones, warm brown eyes, and full lips that Pisces wanted to taste so badly.

"Uh, th-thanks," Peter stuttered. A hint of pink darkened Peter's cheeks, and his smile somehow managed to turn shy. "You, uh, look great, too."

Grinning broadly, Pisces mentally preened at his mate's praise. "Here." He held up the roses. When Peter's black brows shot up and he stared in obvious surprise, Pisces quickly told him, "I didn't really know if you were a flower guy, but my friend encouraged me, and I figured"—Pisces paused a second, shrugging—"couldn't hurt. Right?"

Peter chuckled softly. "No. Can't hurt." He reached out and took them, immediately bringing them to his nose to take a sniff. His smile warmed. "They smell wonderful." With another shy look, Peter admitted, "Never had a guy bring me flowers. Thank you."

Pisces grinned. "Glad you like them."

With a nod, Peter stepped back. "Let me just put these in some water. Then we can leave." He beckoned with his free hand. "I know grandma left behind a couple of vases."

Stepping into the house, Pisces peered around with interest. "Your grandma?" The home had older furnishings, and it obviously hadn't been remodeled in a while, but it appeared clean and gave off warm, welcoming vibes.

"Yeah," Peter confirmed, leading the way down the hallway toward the back. "My grandma left the house to me when she passed." Reaching the kitchen, Peter glanced over his shoulder, a fond expression on his gorgeous features. "That was over six years ago now." His gaze swept over the kitchen's furnishings, pausing on an obviously old and chipped cow cookie jar. "I'm not much for decorating, so other than the master, I kept most everything as is."

"It's very homey," Pisces told him honestly. "I bet you made a lot of fond memories in this place."

"Yeah." Peter's smile turned a little vacant for a few seconds. Then he seemed to shake himself out of whatever thoughts had overtaken him. "So. A vase."

CHAPTER THREE

A s soon as Peter placed the roses in water and gave them one more deep sniff, he thanked Pisces again. Then he led the way out of the house. Peter needed to get the handsome man out of his home before he did something stupid — like beg him to fuck him.

Peter knew Pisces would be more than happy to do it. The hungry expression on the shifter's features — looks he was giving Peter every time he didn't think he was looking — was a dead giveaway. Each time Peter turned back to him, Pisces schooled his features into a warm smile.

Pisces was obviously trying to be a gentleman, which Peter appreciated. While Peter understood the whole shifter-mate dynamic, he wasn't quite ready to just jump in with both feet. He'd watched Colton work hard to win Waylon's affection, and he wanted a little of that.

To that end, Peter led the way out of the house and stopped on the front porch to pull on his jacket. The evenings weren't too cold, yet, but Pisces had warned that he drove an open-topped *Jeep*. Taking in the dark green vehicle, Peter appreciated the warning.

"So, uh, where are we going?" Peter asked curiously.

Pisces took Peter's hand and began leading him to his ride. His fingers were strong and lightly calloused. He squeezed gently before lifting Peter's knuckles to his lips and kissing them, causing the hairs on Peter's arms to stand on end.

"Waylon gave me a couple of ideas," Pisces told him without truly answering. "But if there's something you're in the mood for"—he paused and opened the passenger side door for him—"or not in the mood for, please let me know."

To Peter's surprise, Pisces then helped him into the vehicle. The shifter even leaned into the *Jeep* and buckled his belt for him. The move caused a sliver of discomfort to ease through Peter.

"You know I'm not a girl, right?" Peter scowled a little when he saw Pisces's surprised expression. "I've been buckling my own seatbelt for a long time, Pisces."

Pisces grinned widely, the expression transforming his already handsome features to stunning. His hazel eyes twinkled in the evening light, and his straight white teeth gleamed. After casting a pointed look at Peter's crotch, Pisces met his gaze again and winked.

"Oh, Peter," Pisces rumbled, his expression turning heated. "I know you're not a girl." He focused pointedly at Peter's lap once more, and Peter felt his blood heat and his half-hard prick twitch a bit, threatening to fill. Pisces hummed and licked his lips before focusing on Peter's face again and saying, "Getting your door and taking care of your belt has nothing to do with thinking you're a girl and everything to do with taking care of you, my mate." With a shrug, Pisces told him, "It's a shifter thing, sweetheart. If it bothers you, I'll try to refrain, though."

Peter's blood had begun to burn in response to Pisces's openly hungry looks, and he had to clear his throat in order to manage a response. "Um, well." It suddenly occurred to Peter that he'd never had a boyfriend worried about his health and safety before. It was actually kind of nice. "I may be able to get used to it."

Pisces offered him a winning smile. "Okay." Then he lightly traced his forefingers along Peter's jaw before drawing away and closing the door.

Watching Pisces round the front of the *Jeep*, Peter nibbled his bottom lip. That light, gentle touch made Peter's nipples bead, and he realized he really wanted Pisces to touch him in other places. Peter rubbed his palms on his thighs, trying to get his racing pulse under control.

If this is how Colton made Waylon feel, how did he resist him for so long?

Of course, Waylon had just been getting out of a controlling and manipulative relationship. Colton had understood Peter's friend's need to regroup a little before jumping into another relationship.

"So, uh, what places were you thinking?" Peter asked as Pisces climbed behind the wheel.

The shifter hadn't really said.

"Waylon said you're a fan of seafood," Pisces stated while putting the key in the ignition. He didn't start it, though. Instead, Pisces turned his attention to Peter. "He also said you never say no to Italian, steak, or Mexican. Are you in the mood for something in particular?" Smiling at him, Pisces offered, "Or should I just pick one of my favorites?"

"Well, I had Mexican for lunch," Peter admitted. He'd stopped at a taco truck with Ryley partway through his shift. "But any of the others would be fine."

Pisces nodded once. "Got it." Then he started the *Jeep* and put it into gear. As he peered over his shoulder and backed out of Peter's driveway, he told him, "If you don't mind a short wait, there's an amazing seafood place I know on the pier. Not fancy, but always fresh." Stopping to shift into drive, Pisces winked at him. "Amazing fried calamari."

Peter's mouth began to water. "I love fried calamari." He suddenly wanted it so bad. "I don't mind a wait."

"Sweet." Pisces started them forward. "Let's check it out."

The vehicle was a stick shift, so Pisces kept his hand close, and Peter wondered what the shifter would do if he laid his own hand over it. Peter had never been much of a hand holder, but for some reason, with Pisces, he wanted to try it.

Unfortunately, Peter wasn't quite that brave, yet.

"So is eating seafood like cannibalism for you?" The idea popped into Peter's head, and he was blurting it out before he could think better of it. Instantly, his cheeks began to heat, and he winced. "Uh, never mind."

Pisces glanced his way. The smile curving his lips held a touch of amusement but no ire or censure. "Well, I'm a bottle-nose dolphin shifter, and I don't really know anyone who eats dolphin, so I'm going with no." Letting out a chuckle, he added, "Although, that would be an interesting question to pose to Alpha Kaiser or Beta William."

"What do you mean?" Peter found he appreciated that Pisces didn't just blow him off.

"Well, they both turn into squid," Pisces told him. "Really big ones." His eyes narrowed as he tipped his head to the side a bit, his expression turning musing. "If they eat fried calamari, is it cannibalism?"

It was Peter's turn to bark a soft laugh. "God, it's a strange thought, isn't it?"

Pisces hummed. "It sort of is." He seemed to be running with it, for he added, "Of course, they're a sentient species, and to the best of our knowledge, shifters aren't diced up and tossed into the deep frier."

Peter felt his stomach tighten at that thought. "Oh, god, I would sure hope not."

"I suppose it's like anything. Food quality control," Pisces continued, shaking his head. "But I've seen Eban eat shark-fin soup, and he turns into a great white." Glancing Peter's way, Pisces told him, "I think this is one of those things where it's a matter of opinion, and mine is no, I don't think a shifter eating a non-sentient animal is cannibalism. We're two completely different species."

Nodding absently, Peter replied, "I can see that." Offering the other man a wry smile, he added, "But I think we still need a subject change." Taking in his handsome features and thick, light-brown hair that was just long enough to touch his ears, Peter asked, "So a dolphin shifter." Widening his eyes, he asked, "I just saw the dolphin show at *World of Aquatica*. You said you were there. What were you doing?"

With a broad grin, Pisces glanced his way. "Yup. You saw me perform yesterday afternoon. I was one of the dolphins."

"No shit!" Peter gaped at him for a few seconds before asking, "Were you the one on the right or the left?"

"For most of the show, the one on the right," Pisces told him. "I'm a smidge larger than Angelina, and I'm a slightly darker hue."

Peter scoffed as he thought back to the show. "Wow." Chuckling, he admitted, "I know that the sharks are shifters, but I guess I never thought about the dolphins. Cool."

Pisces found a parking spot and shut off the *Jeep*. Turning to face Peter, he offered him a wry smile. "When I scented you in the stands, I almost botched the show." Pisces smirked as he shook his head. "You were damn distracting."

Warmth flooded Peter, and he smiled at Pisces, but he kept his mouth shut as he slipped from the *Jeep*. He just didn't know what to say to that.

To Pisces's relief, they only had to wait five minutes. They sat on a waiting bench sharing a menu, choosing what they wanted. Pisces couldn't resist putting his arm around Peter, and the smile his mate flashed his way caused his blood to heat and his heart to trip in his chest.

When Pisces's name was called, he was loath to release his mate, so as soon as they stood, he grabbed Peter's hand, instead.

Pisces earned another smile, that time with a slight flush darkening the color of Peter's cheeks.

As soon as they reached their table, Pisces hurried and pulled out Peter's chair. The move earned him another, somewhat surprised-looking smile. As Peter sat and Pisces settled in the chair to his mate's left, he absently wondered what kind of assholes his human must have dated in the past.

Doesn't matter now. He's mine.

With that possessive thought firmly in mind, Pisces relaxed in his chair and eyed the host.

"Can I get you started with anything other than water today?" he offered with a smile and a glance between them. "And your server will be Natalie this evening, and she'll be with you shortly."

"We'd like to get a calamari appetizer started," Peter piped up, pleasing Pisces that he wasn't too shy to express himself. He glanced Pisces's way and asked, "And what bottle of wine did you decide we should split?"

Pisces had mentioned a couple of options while they'd been waiting, and Peter had told him to choose as he'd never gotten the hang of wine pairing.

"Let's go with a bottle of this Riesling." Pisces pointed at his choice on the menu.

The host nodded. "I'll get both of those requests in for you."

After they both murmured their thanks, he hustled away.

"Did you decide on your entrée?" Pisces asked curiously. Peter had mentioned a couple of options. Just to make certain his mate wasn't concerned about price, Pisces added, "I think I'm going to do the surf and turf and add a side of king crab legs."

Peter stared at him wide-eyed for a second, then chuckled. "I'd say I don't know how you'll get through all that, but I know the answer to that."

Pisces winked, knowing the answer, too. Shifters could eat plenty more than the average human. With their body's metabolic rate boosted from shifting forms, they needed many more calories.

Before Peter could offer his choice, their waitress arrived. Natalie carried their bottle of wine, two glasses, and a basket of bread. While placing the glasses on the table, she greeted them and welcomed them to the restaurant. Natalie popped the cork and poured a bit of wine into one of the glasses. Then she glanced between them, asking which of them wanted to sample it.

Considering Pisces already knew he liked the wine, he indicated that she should offer it to Peter. His mate picked up the glass. He made a show of sniffing it before winking at Pisces playfully, and Pisces chuckled, knowing Peter didn't have a clue.

Maybe I'll take him out to a vineyard, and we can do some tastings together . . . see what he likes and doesn't like.

Once Peter took a sip and nodded, he set the glass down. Natalie filled both glasses and set the bottle on the table. Then she asked them if they'd decided or needed another minute.

Pisces arched a brow and shot a questioning look Peter's way.

"Yeah, I think we're ready," Peter confirmed. "I'll take your fried clam strip basket and add on a bowl of clam chowder."

"Of course," Natalie responded before turning to Pisces. "And you, sir?" After Pisces relayed what he wanted, she asked, "What kind of dressing on your salad?"

"I'll take extra ranch," Pisces told her.

Natalie nodded again. "Absolutely." With a smile, she told them, "I'm sure your calamari will be ready in a minute."

After another round of thanks, Natalie hurried away, stopping at a table two down from theirs to help another customer.

Dismissing her for the moment, Pisces picked up his wine glass and took a sip. He set it down and focused on Peter. Pisces racked his brain for something to say, but he'd never

26

been on a date before.

Taking a stab in the dark, Pisces asked, "Have you always wanted to be a paramedic?"

Peter chuckled even as he nodded. "Yup." Grabbing a piece of bread, he began slathering butter on it. "Ever since I was a little boy. I loved watching an ambulance racing down the road, sirens blazing, making everyone else get out of the way." As Peter set the knife down, his smile turned rueful. "Of course, it wasn't until I was older that I realized an ambulance with sirens blazing actually meant trouble for someone." Before taking a big bite of the bread, Peter admitted, "That didn't make me want to do it any less, though."

Pisces chuckled softly as he nodded in understanding. Sometimes, something was just a calling. "How long have you been at it?"

"Nearly six years." Peter cocked his head and eyed Pisces. His voice was low when he commented, "Seen a few things over the years, so finding out about" — he waved his empty hand in the air—"well, it wasn't too shocking." Peter shrugged, holding his gaze. "It actually cleared a few things up."

Humming, Pisces nodded. "I can believe that."

Before he could say more, Natalie returned with their appetizer.

"Thank you." Pisces smiled up at her.

"Certainly, sir." She glanced between them. "Do you need anything else at the moment?"

Peter tapped the side of the appetizer basket. "When you get a moment, will you bring more of the aioli dip, please?"

"You got it." Natalie offered them another winning smile before moving off again.

CHAPTER FOUR

Peter realized it was a little difficult to make certain small talk with Pisces. With him being a shifter, there were so many things he couldn't talk about in public. He couldn't ask simple things, like how old he was or what his duties at *World of Aquatica* were. There was just too great a risk of being overheard.

"Um, so . . ." Peter hesitated as he stabbed a couple of the fried clam strips. As he dipped them in tartar sauce, he asked, "Are your parents around? Uh, have any family?"

Pisces shook his head slowly. "My parents passed some time ago," he told him with a soft smile. "I was an only child, so when that happened, I moved out west."

Biting back his instinctual question of how long ago that was, instead, Peter asked, "Have you worked for Kaiser since the marine park opened?"

Dipping his chin in a quick nod, Pisces revealed, "Since before it opened, actually."

"Huh." Peter wasn't certain how to follow up with that. He had no idea what Kaiser and William did before they'd opened the marine park. In truth, Peter was a little curious about how the brothers had made enough money to buy the land and build the park.

"What about you?" Pisces asked as he carefully pulled the lobster from the tail shell on his plate. Glancing at Peter repeatedly, he expanded, "You mentioned your grandma left you the house, so I'm assuming no grandpa or maybe one in assisted living? Siblings? Parents?" Pausing after cutting the lobster meat into several bites, Pisces focused on him with a look of concern. "Or did your grandma raise you?"

Peter chuckled as he shook his head. "No, my grandparents didn't raise me," he told him. After taking a sip of wine, he continued, "My mom did. Single mother after my dad took off when I was ten."

"I'm sorry."

Shrugging at the standard response, Peter admitted, "Mom was the best, and I don't remember him much." He smiled as he thought of his childhood. "She was smart. Didn't try to keep the house, which she never would have been able to afford on her own." As Peter stabbed more of the tasty, perfectly fried clam strips, he explained, "She found us a nice little condo in the same school district as all my friends, and that way, no yard maintenance, and there was a park nearby. Win, win."

"She sounds like a smart lady," Pisces commented. He dipped his lobster meat into the melted butter. Before popping it into his mouth, Pisces asked, "She still around?"

"Yup, still in the same condo," Peter confirmed. Offering Pisces a mischievous smile, he told him, "And you'll be expected to meet her."

Pisces had just taken a sip of wine, and he coughed roughly for a moment. Placing the wine glass back on the table, he took a couple sips of his water. As Pisces got himself under control, he pinned Peter with an accusatory smile.

Unable to help himself, Peter snickered. "Sorry." Then he shook his head. "No. Not sorry. I shouldn't lie."

"No, you shouldn't lie," Pisces muttered, his voice still sounding a bit rough. After another sip of water, he pinned Peter with a narrow-eyed stare. "So you're close with your mother. Does she know you're gay?"

Peter nodded once. "Well, bisexual, but yeah." Seeing Pisces arch a brow, he shrugged. "I hate labels."

"Understandable." Pisces took a deep breath before letting it out slowly. "So, I get to meet the parents."

Hearing the unease filling Pisces's tone, Peter assured, "It'll be fine, Pisces." When the handsome shifter didn't look convinced, he told him, "All Mom cares about is whether or not you treat me right and if I'm happy." Peter leaned close, lowering his voice, and added, "And considering how your . . . kind behave in a relationship, that won't be an issue. Right?"

Pisces's smile slowly returned. "Correct," he replied just as softly. "You know what you are to me, my mate, and how much I value your happiness and safety."

Peter nodded. "Well, then. Not an issue." He popped a fry into his mouth and smiled at his date.

Narrowing his eyes, Pisces murmured huskily, "Does that mean you accept . . . me?"

Guessing what Pisces was actually asking — was Peter ready to discuss accepting their mating — Peter swallowed . . . hard. He certainly didn't want to lead the man on. He also didn't want to crush the hope he saw shining in Pisces's beautiful hazel eyes.

Except, Peter knew he wasn't quite ready to turn his life upside down and move in with a man he'd just met. He knew that shifters normally did things fast. He'd heard the stories. A couple of shifters would meet, recognize that they were mates, bond, and move in together.

Peter wasn't a shifter, however.

Reaching across the table, Peter rested his hand on Pisces's. He gripped him lightly, enjoying the way Pisces immediately flipped his hand and threaded their fingers. Peter offered the bigger man a warm smile.

"I'm getting there, Pisces," Peter told him. After a second of hesitation, he told him, "I do feel the pull. I really do. And I'm not denying you." After squeezing Pisces's fingers, Peter tried to express his feelings. "I'm just . . . nervous, I guess.

Jumping in with both feet has never been my style, and —"

"It's okay to be nervous, my mate," Pisces rumbled softly, pinning him with an understanding gaze. "You're not the only one who's nervous." Scoffing softly, he smiled. "I've never been in a relationship, and I worry about messing up. Upsetting you." Pisces furrowed his brows as he met Peter's gaze. "Yes, you're my mate, and I want you. Want you by my side, in my bed, and in my arms. But I want you happy, too, so that's why we're going at your speed, so we can learn about each other and discover what makes each of us tick and how to make each other happy." Pisces squeezed Peter's fingers again. "This is okay. You're worth the time."

Relief flooded Peter as he realized that Pisces understood his need for time.

Sure, not having his mate immediately by his side was difficult for Pisces, but he got it. He really did. Peter was human, and even though he knew about shifters, it didn't change his fundamental being.

My mate needs to come to grips with being mine, and he will. There's no rush.

Pisces could be patient. He could give his mate all the time he needed.

"There is just one thing we need to be clear on while we get to know each other," Pisces told him, rubbing his thumb across the back of his hand. "We're exclusive. You don't see anyone else."

Pisces knew himself. If he scented another on his mate, he would hunt the bastard down and gut him. He could never share what Fate deemed his. It just wasn't in his nature.

To Pisces's relief, Peter grinned broadly at him. "That, I can promise you." After another squeeze of his fingers, he stated, "No other but you."

"Damn straight," Pisces muttered.

Peter snickered as he arched one black brow. "Or not so straight."

Catching his meaning, Pisces laughed as he nodded.

A short while later, when Natalie stopped by their table and asked if they needed anything or wanted dessert, they both declined. Pisces asked for the check. As much as Pisces didn't want his time with Peter to end, they couldn't monopolize the table all night.

Once Pisces paid for the meal, he led the way outside. He indicated the boardwalk with his chin and asked, "Do you want to take a stroll after that meal?"

Peter groaned softly while rubbing his belly, and the noise went straight to Pisces's dick. He desperately wanted to hear his mate make those noises for other reasons. Pisces did his best to ignore his quickly filling prick as he waited for Peter's answer.

"With how full I am, it'd probably be a good idea to move a little," Peter admitted, looking around the area. "Let's do a little window shopping."

Pisces turned them to the left and the couple of streets of shops. While Pisces couldn't think of a damn thing he actually needed, he thought it would be a good way to see what interested his mate. Plus, it allowed Pisces to spend more time with Peter.

Taking Peter's hand in his own, Pisces strolled beside the human he hoped to soon make his own. They took their time, wandering down the street and checking out the shops' goods through the windows. Every once in a while, Peter would point out something, and Pisces realized his mate enjoyed items that were cow-themed.

Recalling the cookie jar, Pisces wondered if it had anything to do with his grandma.

Once they'd made it down one street and back up the other, Pisces led the way to his *Jeep*. He again opened his mate's door, helped him in, and buckled his belt. That time, Pisces paid special attention to not only Peter's facial expressions, but the scents he was giving off. He wouldn't continue the activity if it did truly annoy his mate.

Fortunately, Pisces only smelled a hint of amusement from Peter.

Good enough.

Climbing behind the wheel, Pisces started them back toward his mate's home. "Are you working tomorrow?" He probably should have asked earlier.

"I am," Peter confirmed. "Six AM." He grimaced. "My schedule just changed, so it'll take some getting used to."

"When do you get off?" Pisces asked curiously. After a second of hesitation, he offered, "Perhaps I can bring you dinner."

"Typically, I work ten-hour days unless I get a last-minute call that makes us stay late," Peter explained. "So with an hour lunch, I get off at five. Four days on and three days off, so I don't mind."

Pisces nodded slowly. "Damn," he muttered, checking the clock on his dash. It was already after nine. "Sorry I kept you out so late." *Sort of.* "How about I bring you dinner tomorrow to make it up to you. We can eat in."

Peter only hesitated a second before nodding. "Okay." He smiled at Pisces while placing his hand over Pisces's where it rested on the gear shift. "I'd like that."

Lifting his thumb, Pisces rubbed it along the side of Peter's hand. The fact that his mate was reaching out to him caused his heart to race in his chest. He reveled in the fact that Peter was coming to accept him.

Pisces pulled into Peter's driveway and parked. After shutting off the engine, he escorted his mate to the door. He rested his hand on the small of his back, needing the contact as he knew his time with his mate was about to come to an end.

When Peter opened the door, he glanced over his shoulder

with a smile. "Gonna give me a goodbye kiss?" he asked as he stepped into his foyer.

Unable to resist that offering, Pisces stepped in behind him and closed the door. He turned his mate even as he slid his arms around his waist. Lifting one hand, Pisces cradled Peter's jaw.

Meeting Peter's warm, brown-eyed gaze, Pisces felt a spike of lust rush through his veins. The way his mate licked his bottom lip as if in anticipation was like a siren's call. Pisces quickly dipped his head, sealing his mouth over Peter's.

Pisces groaned softly at the feel of Peter's lips beneath his own. Sliding his hand along his jaw, he pressed his thumb into the corner of his mate's mouth. Under the light pressure, Peter opened to him, and Pisces took full advantage.

Slipping his tongue into Peter's mouth, Pisces enjoyed the heady taste of his mate, and just like the first time, it damn near rocked his world. He teased along his human's appendage as he savored the mixture of food, wine, and something all Peter's own. As Pisces's tongue danced with Peter's, his mate pressing into the kiss and giving as good as he got, Pisces felt tingles racing down his spine.

Tightening the arm Pisces had around Peter's waist, he felt the press of a firm erection against his own. He bucked his hips, unable to help himself. Peter fed him a moan and mirrored the move, rutting against him.

When Peter's strong hands gripped Pisces's biceps in a firm grip, he feared he'd gone too far. Instead of pushing him away, however, his mate clutched him closer. Pisces felt Peter writhe in his hold as if he wanted to crawl beneath his skin.

Tearing his mouth away, Peter turned his head and whined his name. "Pisces." He shuddered and bucked in Pisces's hold, clearly not trying to get away.

Pisces groaned and lowered his mouth to Peter's neck. Sealing his lips over the flesh where his neck met his shoulder, he began to suck and nibble. He wanted to sink his teeth in and start their bond so very badly, and he knew if he didn't stop, he might lose control.

"Oh, god, Pisces," Peter whined even as he continued to move against him. "C-Close."

With a growl, Pisces sank to his knees. He rested his hands on Peter's belt and peered up at his soon-to-be lover. Knowing he needed permission, he asked, "May I suck you, my mate?"

Peter's nostrils flared, and he stared down at him with heavy-lidded eyes. His kiss-swollen lips were parted as he panted for breath.

Sucking in a sharp breath, Peter jerked a nod. "Hell, yeah." His hips bucked a little, his mate searching for stimulation. "Fuckin' suck me, Pisces."

Pisces didn't wait for a second invitation. He made quick work of Peter's belt, button, and fly. With a quick tug, he had his mate's jeans and briefs partway down his thighs.

Spotting Peter's long, slender erection jutting from his groin, Pisces only took a few seconds to admire the cut piece of meat. He spotted the bead of pre-cum gleaming at the tip and saw the way the swollen red length danced before him. Opening his mouth, Pisces quickly swallowed Peter to the root.

Peter groaned his pleasure, his back arching, pushing into Pisces's sucking hold. Pisces gripped his mate's hips, allowing him a little control. Then he began working his mate's maybe seven-inch length.

Pisces sucked strongly as he pulled partway off, enjoying the feel of his girth on his tongue. After swiping his tongue over the crown and tapping at the nerves beneath it, he sank back down. Inhaling noisily through his nose, Pisces reveled in the masculine aroma of his mate in the throes of needing.

He lodged Peter's crown in the back of his throat and swallowed. Hearing Peter shout his name, Pisces peered up at his mate through his lashes and did it again.

With Peter's head thrown back, his neck flushed with his pleasure, and his swollen lips parted on his cry, Pisces had never seen anything more gorgeous in his life.

A shudder to Peter's body followed by his whimper was the only warning Pisces got before his mate erupted, filling his throat with his seed. He swallowed quickly as he eased partway off, allowing the next burst to land on his tongue. The sharp flavor of his mate's spunk lit up Pisces's taste buds and quickly went to his head.

Pisces swallowed again, sucked for more, and then lost all control as his balls pulled tight. Untouched, he shot in his pants, his senses singing with bliss.

CHAPTER FIVE

"You've been awfully quiet today," Ryley commented, drawing Peter's attention. He and his fellow paramedic sat in the back of their ambulance doing inventory. When Peter met Ryley's gaze, his coworker smirked at him. "And a lot of the time, you've had this sappy smile on your face."

Peter scowled at his friend. "I have not," he countered, returning his attention to his own list.

"Uh, yeah. You have." Ryley used the back of his clipboard to tap Peter's upper arm. "You meet someone?"

Their day had started first thing with a call about a man having a heart attack and hadn't slowed down for the first five hours. Running into hour six, they were finally able to take a breather. It was a good thing, too, because there were a few things they needed to stock up on.

Plus, Peter knew he hadn't been the only one hungry. They'd grabbed some sandwiches from a sub shop and had eaten fast. Then they chose to use the rest of their lunch hour to restock.

Unable to deny Pisces — that would just have been a rotten thing to do — Peter dipped his chin in a nod. "I did have a date last night," he admitted.

"Ahhhh, now we're getting somewhere," Ryley responded with a chuckle. "And from the smile, it must have gone well." When Peter didn't respond, Ryley asked, "Man or woman?"

His paramedic partner knew he was bisexual.

"Man," Peter confirmed.

Peter hopped out of the back of the ambulance and headed

to the supply closet. After counting out the necessary items and noting on the chart what he'd taken, he returned. Peter quickly had the items put away securely. Then he updated his own list.

"A good one, obviously." Ryley snorted as he hopped down from the ambulance. In the same tone as if he were discussing the weather, Ryley asked, "You get blown?"

For a second, Peter didn't process Ryley's question. When he did, he snapped his head up and stared at his coworker with wide eyes. "Ryley." He gasped indignantly, even as he began to feel heat start to work its way up his neck.

Ryley was walking backward, his attention pinned on him, obviously waiting for a reaction. Barking a laugh, he grinned broadly. "You did." Ryley cackled as he pointed at Peter's blush. "Damn, Peter. You dog, you."

"Fuck, Ryley." Peter shook his head in shock. "Anyone listening would think that *you* were the one under thirty, not me."

With a dismissive wave, Ryley turned to focus on where he was going even as he called over his shoulder, "I'm thirty-six, not dead."

Peter shook his head as he finished up his chart before tucking it away. Slipping from the back, he started walking around the vehicle, checking for problems. Just because they were paramedics didn't mean he and Ryley didn't do their best to make certain their ambulance was always in tip-top mechanical shape.

Even a blown tire could turn into a life-and-death situation, so Peter checked treads and air pressure religiously.

Ryley returned and hopped in the back to put away whatever he'd gotten. He was just closing a drawer when Peter returned around back.

Without missing a beat, Ryley pried, "So, what's the name of this guy?"

"Pisces," Peter answered.

Arching a brow, Ryley repeated, "Pisces?" Peter nodded, and Ryley commented, "Interesting name. Pisces what?"

Peter paused. "Uhhh . . . I don't know?"

"How long have you been dating?" Ryley asked with a scoff.

Nibbling his bottom lip, Peter really didn't want to tell his coworker that it'd been a first date.

Ryley put away his clipboard and refocused fully on him with narrowed eyes. "Really? First date?" he guessed. When Peter again kept his mouth shut, Ryley rolled his eyes. "Blown on a first date by a guy named Pisces." Ryley smirked. "Sure it wasn't just a hook-up?"

Peter could see how Ryley would think that, but he still shook his head. "No. He's bringing me supper tonight."

At that revelation, Ryley appeared surprised. "Seein' the guy two nights in a row." He eased to sit on the tailgate and gazed at Peter steadily. "You must really like this guy."

After taking a deep breath, Peter let it out slowly with a nod. "Yeah. Yeah, I do."

Ryley patted him on the shoulder. "Well, I hope it goes well for you. Everyone needs a—"

The dispatcher's voice over the loudspeaker interrupted Ryley. Hearing their ambulance number, Ryley hopped down. After securing the rear doors, they hurried to the front, jumped in, and got moving with Ryley behind the wheel.

The code for the call was assault in progress, so they weren't surprised when they spotted the police vehicles. When Ryley stopped behind one, they both exited. While Ryley went to talk to one of the boys in blue, Peter headed to the back to open their doors.

Ryley returned with an officer who appeared vaguely familiar.

When Peter heard the name Officer McKellan, he offered,

"Hello again, officer." He'd met the man on several occasions. He was fairly new to one of Sacramento's precincts, but Peter figured he would become more familiar with him as time went on. "What do we have?"

"Another one of those damn biting assaults," Officer McKellan grumbled, frowning while rubbing the back of his neck. "At least this time, we're gettin' a description of the guy by the person who called it in."

Well, damn. That could be dangerous. If the rogue vamp finds out who ratted him out, he could end up in the guy's crosshairs.

As discreetly as possible, using the gurney to hide his movements, Peter shot off a quick text to Pisces. His shifter could check out the scene while it was fresh. Maybe that would help him.

My shifter?

Huh. I kinda like the sound of that.

Peter shoved his phone back into his pocket just as they reached the downed woman. She wore a dark-blue dress suit and was leaning up against the brick wall. Considering she only wore one shoe and the other one was near the opening of the alley, Peter figured she'd been dragged.

Gazing at the officer beside her with a dazed expression, she appeared to be blinking and trying to focus. That was something. It meant the rogue had been interrupted.

Ryley kept his voice soft and soothing as he introduced them. He needed to ask her name three times, but she finally managed to tell it to them—Marrisa Engleman. She was a thirty-two-year-old business executive who'd just left a lunch meeting. Marrisa couldn't recall what day it was, and considering the open wound on her neck, they would definitely have to take her in.

After they loaded Marrisa onto the gurney and were getting her comfortable, she began to flail about in agitation.

"What's wrong, Marrisa?" Ryley asked, rubbing her shoulder in an attempt to soothe her. "Do you hurt somewhere else now?"

"My purse," Marrisa mumbled, trying to sit up and look for it. "Where's m'purse?"

"I didn't see a purse, ma'am," the officer claimed. "I'm sorry. Your attacker must have taken it."

"N-No." Marrisa continued to look. "Need it." Frowning at the officer, she claimed, "M'daughter's marbles are in there."

Oooookay.

Peter wondered if Marrisa wasn't a few marbles short herself. Still, as Ryley began wheeling her gurney while trying to assure her that they would look, Peter and the officer began searching. While Peter went a little deeper in the alley, the officer headed toward a nearby dumpster.

Reaching the end, Peter was just about to turn around when a metallic flash caught his attention. He jogged a few yards closer and realized he was indeed looking at a woman's purse. Knowing better than to touch possible evidence, Peter began to turn away, intending to call for the officer.

After only two steps, Peter felt a strong arm wrap around his chest and yank him back against a firm torso. His gut clenched as he smelled the unmistakable aroma of old, dried blood. When a nose pressed against his neck, Peter couldn't help but shake as fear slithered through him.

"Oooohhhh, now don't you smell good, little human," the vampire purred darkly into his ear. "You were a shifter snack not too long ago. I can still smell him on you. Now you can be a snack for me."

Peter felt his brain freeze for one heartbeat, then two. Feeling the scrape of the vampire's fangs as he skimmed them up his neck jerked him from his stasis. Even though his panicking brain supplied that it was probably too late, Peter screamed.

Pulling out his phone, Pisces checked his text. He read Peter's message and smiled.

Call on Fourth and McGyver. Another one. Want to check a fresh scene?

Pisces looked at the lights flashing down the road . . . near Fourth and McGyver. Unbeknownst to Peter, he'd been verifying his movements all day. Of course, his mate wasn't the only paramedic he'd followed.

After Ovram set up a police band radio in his *Jeep* that morning, Pisces had headed into town. He knew from their pod's tech guru what Peter's ambulance handle was. Ovram had also given him a list of first responder codes.

To that end, any time something was called in, Pisces had known about it. He verified who it was, where they were going, and the reason why. Any time someone was sent to a possible assault or robbery, Pisces tailed them.

Pisces would explain later why he was so close. Instead of responding via text, he slid out of his vehicle and began walking toward the scene. He saw a paramedic wheeling a gurney toward the ambulance, but he didn't see Peter.

Having no desire to possibly get Peter into trouble, Pisces moved down a side street. He ducked into another alley and began looking for a way to access the area from the back. Because he already had the vampire's scent, Pisces hoped to be able to pick up the rogue's fresh trail as he ran from the scene.

Just as Pisces thought he caught a whiff of the vamp's scent, a blood-curdling scream rent the air. Recognizing the voice, he felt his gut clench. Bursting into a sprint, Pisces rounded a corner, and what he spotted made his blood run cold.

Peter was held in the grip of an unkempt lanky man. Stringy hair fell across his features, but Pisces could make out his blood-red eyes as the vampire stared at his mate's jugular. A smile curved his open lips, showcasing fangs ready to pierce Peter's throat.

"Get away from him," Pisces roared, surging forward once

more. He was only a few yards away, and he ran for all he was worth, but he feared he would still be too late.

The vampire snapped his attention to him just as Peter crumpled. After a glance at his fallen prey, the rogue sprinted in the other direction. Paranormal fast, he practically flew past a startled cop, who was probably also responding to Peter's scream. Then the vampire disappeared around the corner and out of sight.

"Peter," Pisces cried, dropping to his knees beside his mate. Gripping his shoulders, he tugged his human onto his lap. "Peter? Are you okay?" Threading his fingers through Peter's hair, then down his neck, Pisces checked both sides. "Peter, can you hear me?"

"Sir, put the paramedic down and step away from him."

Hearing the bellowed order, Pisces snapped his attention away from Peter. He saw the officer pointing the gun at the ground a few feet away from them and just bit back his growl. Scowling at the man, Pisces snarled, "Seriously?"

"Pisces?" Peter's whisper redrew Pisces's attention back to his mate.

"Hi, sweetheart," Pisces murmured, doing his best to keep his voice calm. "You scared the shit out of me."

Peter looked dazed and confused. "What are you doing here?"

"You texted me," Pisces replied. "Remember?"

"Peter?" The officer approached, still holding his weapon at the ready. "Do you know this man?"

After blinking a couple of times, Peter seemed to start processing things a little better. "Yeah. Pisces is my boyfriend," Peter claimed, causing a swell of pride to rush through Pisces. He glanced around. "Where's the vam—" Peter snapped his mouth shut. Lifting his gaze to the officer, he claimed, "Officer McKellan, there was another man here. The guy who attacked Marrisa." Furrowing his brows in obvious confusion, he muttered, "Pisces must have scared him away."

"There was a guy who looked homeless fleeing the scene," Officer McKellan stated, finally holstering his weapon. "You think he's our perp?"

Peter nodded, then began to move as if intending to stand. "Yeah. Definitely."

"Well, shit." A muscle ticked in Officer McKellan's jaw as he rested his hands on his hips and shook his head. "That guy flew outta here like a bat outta hell. Never seen anyone move so fast."

Pisces made a mental note to talk to Alpha Kaiser about this guy. It was possible they would need to do a little damage control — maybe a memory adjustment.

As Peter continued to make as if to stand, Pisces quickly moved to help him. He didn't like the way his mate seemed so unsteady. Keeping a grip on one arm, Pisces offered Peter his support.

"Are you okay, sweetheart?" Pisces asked again.

Peter slowly nodded his head while resting one hand against a wall. Using his chin, he indicated a purse lying nearby. "I was going to come find you, officer, when he grabbed me." Then Peter seemed to gain enough strength to push off the wall and stand on his own. "That guy was definitely going to bite me like he did Marrisa. Said I smelled good." He seemed to catch himself again and pointed at the purse. "Anyway, I think that's Marrisa's purse, but I didn't want to touch it if it's evidence."

"Good call, Peter," Officer McKellan stated with a slight nod. "I'll collect it. Then I'll need your statement about the attack." After a glance between them, the officer added, "As well as the best description I can get from you two."

Well, shit. So much for chasing a fresh scent.

Hopefully, by the time Pisces was finished, the trail wouldn't have been too disrupted.

After all, seeing to my mate's welfare always comes first.

CHAPTER SIX

"You sure you're okay to finish out your shift?" Ryley stared at him with worry in his dark eyes.

Peter nodded. "Yeah." He patted his partner's arm. "I'll be okay." Then he climbed into the back with Marrisa, who was only too happy to have her purse back.

Evidently, due to the fabric being impossible to get prints off of, Officer McKellan had returned it to her without delay.

Ryley took Peter at face value and closed the doors.

Peter spent the ride keeping an eye on Marrisa while doing a few deep breathing exercises of his own. He didn't know what shocked him more — getting snagged by the vampire or having Pisces turn up to save him. Peter would definitely have some questions about that, but he knew that at the scene was not the appropriate time.

Fortunately, Pisces seemed to realize it, too. He'd pecked a hard kiss to Peter's lips, then let him go.

After leaving Marrisa in the hospital staff's care, Peter and Ryley climbed in the back of the ambulance to prep it for the next call.

"Sooooo." Ryley grinned at Peter. "That was one-date-blowjob guy, huh?" He waggled his eyebrows playfully. "Pisces, no last name."

"Well, at least now I know his last name," Peter replied, although he figured Pisces's last name wasn't really Ratherton, no matter what his driver's license said.

Ryley sobered as he nodded. "You shouldn't have been in that alley," he grumbled. "It should have been another cop.

You should have been safely with me."

Peter shrugged. "Probably right." Resting his hand on Ryley's upper arm, he gave it a squeeze. "But we can't change what happened, so how about we concentrate on the fact that I'm okay. Hmm?"

After blowing out another huff, Ryley nodded. "Fair enough."

They only had one call after that, and they were able to clean and restock their ambulance with plenty of time to finish paperwork and clock out on time.

"Doing anything fun on your three days off?" Ryley asked, his grin lascivious. "Other than Pisces, of course."

"Ryley, you are way too interested in my love life, man," Peter stated with a laugh. "I really think you need to go out and get laid."

With a grunt, Ryley looked away, the mirth sliding from his features.

"Hey." Standing in the evening sun outside the ambulance bay, Peter gripped Ryley's upper arm. "What's wrong?"

Using his other hand to rub the back of his neck, Ryley met Peter's gaze. "I've tried a few times, but I just can't seem to find anyone that makes my prick perk up."

Ryley mumbled the words so quietly that Peter was surprised he managed to hear them.

After a quick glance around, Peter kept his voice low when he asked, "You havin' trouble getting it up?" Knowing erectile dysfunction was a damn sensitive subject for most men, he quickly murmured, "There's medication for that now."

With a quick shake of his head, Ryley tipped his head and started them walking again. He didn't say anything until he reached his SUV. Then he leaned against it and shoved his hands into his pockets.

"Not havin' that kind of trouble," Ryley claimed, a frown marring his features as he glanced from Peter to the ground and back again. "Just can't find any ladies that interest me." Before Peter could ask if maybe he needed new hunting grounds, Ryley scoffed and muttered, "But there was this one guy that—" He shook his head. "Yeah, that was a shocker, right there."

Peter thought he was starting to understand. "You know, even at your age, it's okay to experiment." When Ryley squinted at him, he teased, "After all. You said it. You're thirty-six, not that old."

Scoffing, Ryley shook his head. "I wouldn't even know where to begin."

Slapping his hands together and rubbing his palms, Peter grinned broadly. "Oh, boy, have you come to the right place." With a wink, he pointed at Ryley. "Okay, I have plans to go sailing with Pisces tomorrow, but the day after, I'm gonna have an impromptu barbeque. Come. Me and my friends can help you out."

Ryley's face turned a pinkish hue. "I don't know," he hedged.

"No excuses, or we're comin' to get you," Peter declared, continuing to point at him. He started toward his own vehicle even as he called, "Day after tomorrow, Ryley."

By the time Peter had reached his *Cherokee*, Ryley still hadn't responded. He opened the door and stood on the running board. Peering over the top of the door, Peter gave Ryley a hard look.

Finally, Ryley nodded once. Then his coworker disappeared into his SUV. With a grin, still a little blown away, he slipped into his ride, more than ready to get home.

As badly as Pisces had wanted to, he'd managed to keep his hands to himself the prior evening—mostly, anyway. After feeding Peter a dinner of pizza, hot wings, and cheesy bread—after his mate's rough day, Pisces figured a little comfort food was in order—he curled up on the sofa with him and watched a movie. Pisces had seen his lover yawning, so it certainly helped him control his ardor.

Instead, Pisces had restricted their sexual activities to quite a bit of necking, followed by mutual hand jobs. After he'd cleaned them up, they'd cuddled some more. Peter had been out like a light.

After the movie ended, Pisces had put Peter to bed and managed to do the gentlemanly thing and hadn't crawled in after him. He'd gone home.

It had sucked, but he kept reminding himself that he was meeting his mate the next day.

Now, the next day is here.

Pisces parked his *Jeep* in the marina parking lot. A couple of years prior, Peter had gotten into sailing. He'd bought a small boat and rented a slip.

While Pisces had never been sailing, he couldn't wait to share one of Peter's passions.

Grabbing his backpack, Pisces slung it over his shoulder and closed up his *Jeep*. He had absolutely no valuables in the open-topped vehicle. Pisces even had one of those radios with a removable face plate, making it useless to steal.

Striding down the boat ramp, Pisces swept his gaze over the myriad of boats filling the marina. He saw many different designs and sail configurations, and he wondered which one was Peter's. Pisces also wondered what was the point of so many.

I figure if I say a sailboat is a sailboat, some enthusiast is going to have an aneurysm.

As long as it's not my Peter.

With a chuckle under his breath, Pisces knew that thought wasn't true. He had enough of a brain to know that different styles were used for different purposes. There were racing boats, sailboats, skiffs, and dinghies. Hell, anyone watching old pirate movies would recognize names like schooners, galleons, and maybe even cutters.

Pisces paused near the opening and tipped his head back. Inhaling deeply, he tried to pick up some scent of his mate. Unfortunately, with the light breeze, all Pisces smelled was the salty sea air.

Not that that's a bad thing. I love salty sea air. I am a dolphin, after all.

"Hey, Pisces!"

Hearing Peter's call, Pisces turned and spotted him on another part of the walkway. He backtracked a little before turning onto a platform that accessed that area. As Pisces strode to his waiting mate, he admired Peter's handsome body.

Peter wore a pair of vibrant blue board shorts with a red tank top. His hair was covered by a floppy-brimmed hat. While his eyes were hidden by shades, he sported a large smile, which caused Pisces's pulse to race within him.

When Pisces's dick had the predictable reaction—starting to plump—he decided to check out the boat instead. The hull was black and maybe thirty feet from stem to stern. There was a single mast near the front where the sail was currently furled. The back space appeared roomy, and Pisces bet Peter had bought it with the idea in mind of being able to take out friends.

Lucky me. I'm that friend today.

"Permission to come aboard, captain," Pisces teased, pausing on the dock beside the boat.

With a laugh, Peter nodded. "Permission granted."

Carefully, Pisces climbed into the boat. He stumbled a little as it rocked beneath his feet. He quickly caught his balance and made his way over to Peter.

"Good morning, my mate," Pisces rumbled as he slipped his arms around Peter's waist.

Pisces didn't bother asking permission. He decided to assume he already had it. Peter's hands immediately going to his chest was a pretty good giveaway.

Lowering his head, Pisces sealed his mouth over Peter's. He nipped and licked at his lips for a moment before pushing his tongue deep. Pisces hummed in appreciation at his mate's delicious flavor—a flavor he knew he would never get enough of.

Hearing a wolf whistle followed by someone hollering, "Get a room," Pisces pulled back.

Ignoring the callers, Pisces grinned down at his mate. "You always taste wonderful, my mate." He gave his mate a wicked smile. "Never gonna get tired of it, and gonna do it as often as you'll let me."

"Well, since you're such a good kisser, I suppose I could allow it often."

Pisces laughed heartily upon hearing Peter's playfulness. Lowering his hand, he smacked his mate's butt before giving the cheek an appreciative squeeze. With a wink, he pulled away.

"Well, if you don't want me to scandalize the natives, we better get moving," Pisces told him. Glancing around, he asked, "Can I help?"

"Have you ever sailed before?" Peter asked, taking a step away from him.

Pisces shook his head. "You'd think that, as someone who's over a hundred and thirty years old, I'd have done it at least once, but nope." He grinned and shrugged. "I would just swim from place to place."

"Makes sense," Peter conceded. Pointing to the bench seat at the back, he told him, "Just sit, relax, and stay out of my way." He grinned and winked, softening his order.

Obeying, Pisces settled in the seat. He watched Peter in action, unfurling the mast and adjusting the tension. After untying their moors, Peter grabbed the wheel in one hand and some kind of handle attached to the sail with the other. In short order, he had the sailboat drifting out of the marina.

"Damn, that's impressive," Pisces commented, impressed.

"Just takes a little training and practice," Peter told him, but the pleased smile on his face told Pisces that his mate liked the praise.

"You must go out sailing often then." Pisces relaxed in his seat, watching the waves roll by. "Because you look damn skilled."

Peter graced him with another pleased smile. "Often enough."

Pisces was content to watch for a while, enjoying the sea breeze on his face. The view was fantastic, too. He loved seeing the happiness on Peter's face as he navigated them north up the coast.

"Thanks for letting me pass out on you last night," Peter finally said, ending the silence. He glanced over at him, his lips twisting in a rueful smile. "It'd been an eventful day."

"It certainly wasn't any hardship, Peter," Pisces told him warmly. "I'll always take any opportunity to hold you and care for you." He allowed his voice to grow more serious. "You know that. You're my mate."

Humming, Peter flashed another smile his way. "I know." His chest expanded as he took in a deep breath. Then he let it out through pursed lips. "And . . . I've been doing a lot of thinking, and I'd like you to claim me this evening."

Pisces's half-hard prick became hard as a rock in seconds. Groaning, he pressed the heel of one hand to his groin. "Damn, sweetheart." He hissed at the pressure. "You say that now when we're in the middle of the ocean, and I can't do a damn thing to you?"

Peter lowered his sunglasses and peered at him over the rims. "Well, if you know of some private cove up here, maybe we could do something about it."

Issuing a low growl, Pisces quickly thought about all the

secluded places along the coastal waters owned by *World of Aquatica.* "I think I can point out a few places." Seeing Peter's hungry smile, he asked, "You ever sailed up that way before?"

Shaking his head, Peter admitted, "Nope. I normally go south for the fishing."

"Well, it'll be a new experience for you then," Pisces rumbled, lust and need swelling through him. Looking at the shoreline, he wondered how long it would take to get to the pod's territory by sea.

"You know what else would be a new experience?"

At Peter's question, Pisces focused on his mate. "What's that?"

Peter grinned at him. "I've never sailed with a dolphin before."

Chuckling, Pisces leaned forward and whipped his shirt over his head. "Now that." He kicked out of his sandals. "Is something I can remedy." After a quick glance around to make certain there weren't any other close boats, he shucked his shorts, leaving him naked. "Right now."

The soft whimpering moan Peter let out told Pisces just how much his mate enjoyed the sight of his naked body. He couldn't very well do anything about his erection, but Peter didn't seem to mind, considering his attention was riveted on Pisces's hard dick. Still sitting on the seat, Pisces spread his legs a little and gave his nearly ten-inch cock a stroke.

"See something you like?" Pisces teased.

Peter moaned as he rolled his eyes. "Duh."

Pisces laughed again. "Okay. Let's go play."

After another quick look around, Pisces slipped over the boat railing and into the water. He winked at his mate before sinking beneath the waves. His shift was short and quick, and before long, he was rising to the surface in his bottlenose dolphin form.

Coming up to the side of the boat, Pisces swam alongside. He loved the way Peter laughed, and how he leaned over and petted him was even better. Then, with a swish of his powerful tail, Pisces propelled himself toward the bow of the sailboat.

With a leap, Pisces cleared the waves, showing off for his mate.

CHAPTER SEVEN

While Peter had often enjoyed sailing alone, he could never remember when he'd enjoyed it so much. Perhaps it was because he wasn't truly alone. Instead, the sexy shifter he was coming to feel great emotions for was playfully frolicking in the waters around his boat.

In his dolphin form, Pisces was sleek and beautiful. He exuded power and elegance. Pisces easily leaped out of the waves, danced across the surface, and twirled in the air.

Peter knew he would never grow tired of watching him.

Just as Pisces's dolphin began veering to the right, leading Peter toward shore and a secluded cove there, movement to his left caught his attention. He spotted a large dorsal fin break the surface, and it began moving in their direction. The body beneath the water appeared long and black.

Watching the large marine creature crest the waves, Peter realized what he was seeing—an orca. Then he recalled another name for them—killer whales. Gaping, Peter swept his gaze over the ocean, looking for Pisces.

Didn't orcas sometimes eat dolphins?

"Pisces," Peter shouted, searching frantically.

As if responding to his call, Pisces leaped out of the water and chittered. He must have seen what Peter did, but instead of retreating, his lover surged toward the orca. Shaking his head in disbelief, Peter watched Pisces lunge from the water, twist in mid-air, and splash down sideways near the much, much larger marine animal.

Looks like a kid in a pool body-splashing another.

When the orca twisted around and used the flat of its massive tail to splash Pisces back, Peter understood.

The orca was a shifter, too.

They're playing together.

Laughing in disbelief, Peter watched them for several minutes. Finally, the orca bumped noses with Pisces and began moving back toward open sea. Pisces headed back to Peter.

By the time Pisces reached Peter's sailboat, he'd returned to his human form. He hung on the side of the boat and grinned up at him.

"You scared the shit out of me," Peter blurted with a shake of his head and a glance toward the orca's retreating body. "I thought it was going to eat you."

Pisces chuckled even as he heaved himself back into the boat. "Naw," he countered, grabbing a towel and quickly wrapping it around his waist. *Too bad.* "That's Seri, a buddy of mine. I'll introduce you to him another time."

Blowing out a breath, Peter nodded even as his heartrate began to spike for a wholly different reason. A wet, naked Pisces was truly a sight to see. He couldn't help but lick his lips as he watched rivulets of water trickle down Pisces's expansive torso.

"Yeah. Okay," Peter murmured absently, his gaze tracking over Pisces's firm bronzed flesh. "Figured he was when you started playing."

Humming, Pisces sidled up into Peter's space. Cradling Peter's jaw in one wet hand, he rumbled, "You were worried about me?"

Peter felt his blood heat in his veins as he stared into Pisces's hungry hazel eyes. He had to swallow, hard, to find his tongue. "Yeah," Peter whispered. "Of course, I was."

Pisces's nostrils flared, and his expression turned heavy-lidded. Lowering his head, he pressed a soft, wet kiss to Peter's lips. Instead of taking it deep, as Peter had hoped, Pisces lifted his head and took a step backward.

Pointing toward the shore, Pisces told him, "There's a little secluded cove you can anchor in right there." His features took on a feral cast. "Then I can show you how much I appreciate your concern."

A ripple of anticipation worked through Peter. His nipples beaded, and his stomach clenched. Blood rushed south so fast that he was certain his swaying wasn't caused just by the movement of the waves.

Tearing his gaze away from Pisces, Peter nodded. "Yeah," he responded roughly. "Okay."

Peter felt his hands tremble even as he guided his sailboat through the waves. Keeping a sharp eye on everything around them, he made certain to keep away from any possible obstructions. Finally, Peter had his boat tucked around the corner of the outcroppings Pisces indicated, shielding them from view, and he furled the sails and dropped the anchor.

With a wave of anticipation flooding him, Peter turned toward Pisces. His lover had already spread several towels over the boat's decking. He'd even pulled a throwable rescue cushion onto the floor as a makeshift pillow.

Pisces had also ditched the towel. He stood watching Peter, his hand gripped around his erection. Jacking himself slowly, Pisces stared at him with heat burning in his eyes.

"Ready to be mine, Peter?" Pisces asked on a growl.

Feeling his own prick twitch in his shorts, Peter replied, "I thought I already was yours."

Grinning widely, Pisces claimed, "You are, but that doesn't mean I don't long for you to wear my mark for all the world to see." His gaze slid to Peter's shoulder, and he licked his lips. "And our life-threads will be connected. Mine to yours, and yours to mine. One in all ways."

Peter's anticipation ramped up, and he sidled closer to his waiting lover. "I'm looking forward to it," he admitted.

Reaching down, Peter gently batted Pisces's hand away from his cock. "And that means." He wrapped his fingers around his shifter's erection and gave it a light stroke. "This is mine."

Pisces groaned deeply, and his hips bucked. "Yesssss," he hissed, bringing his hands up to grip Peter's upper arms. "Your touch is so damn good."

"I bet this will be better," Peter claimed before sinking to his knees.

Unable to wait an instant longer, Peter opened his mouth and wrapped his lips around Pisces's wide head. As Pisces moaned Peter's name, he groaned his own pleasure upon experiencing his first taste of the shifter. His lover's cock was thick and heavy on his tongue with a deep, robust flavor. Sinking deeper, Peter took him as far as he could go before needing to back off. He'd never blown anyone as long as Pisces, and he knew he would need to work up to it.

I'll damn sure enjoy the practice, though.

Peter peered up at Pisces when he felt his lover slide his fingers into his hair. His lover stared down at him with undeniable need etched across his handsome features. Smiling around Pisces's tasty flesh, Peter moved one hand to the base of his lover's cock and squeezed.

Pisces's nostrils flared, and he sucked in a sharp breath. He gave an experimental thrust. When Peter hummed appreciatively, Pisces took that as the permission it was.

Tightening his grip on Peter's head, Pisces began a series of swift, sharp ruts. His breathing sped up, his lips parted, and he panted heavily. His chest heaved, flushing dark. Pisces's eyes dilated widely as he obviously chased his pleasure, fucking Peter's mouth almost mindlessly.

Wanting to taste Pisces's seed so badly, Peter moved his second hand from his lover's thigh to his testicles. He gently cradled the heavy orbs, earning a barking groan from Pisces's throat. When he squeezed lightly, Pisces appeared to vibrate.

Then Peter felt it. Pisces's balls lifted from his palm, drawing tight. Peter hummed, sucking hard, offering every bit of stimulation he could.

Pisces tipped back his head and roared while thrusting one last time. His body shook as he sank as deep as Peter's hand on his base would allow. Thick bursts of cum flooded Peter's mouth, landing on his tongue.

Peter swallowed, sucked, and swallowed some more. His shifter's seed tasted better than anything he could ever remember. He'd always enjoyed sucking cock, and Peter knew that blowing Pisces would soon become one of his favorite past times.

Oh, yeah.

As soon as Pisces stopped spurting, he jerked back, yanking his prick from Peter's mouth. His dick still appeared hard and was even twitching at his groin. Seed continued to dribble from his slit.

Pisces didn't give Peter a chance to lick him clean. Instead, he sank to his knees and pounced. Grabbing the sides of Peter's tank top, Pisces growled and pulled.

The sound of fabric tearing filled the air, Pisces rending it from Peter's body. The obvious, feral need emanating from his shifter sent Peter's pulse soaring. He stared at the pieces of his shirt in shock, even as his balls tingled at the feral display.

"Holy shit," Peter whispered.

"Need you," Pisces rumbled, pushing Peter back onto the towels. He grabbed the waistband of Peter's board shorts and began tugging them down his legs, and Peter lifted his hips accommodatingly. Pisces growled as he quickly stripped Peter of his clothes, saying, "Need you now, my mate."

"Yes, Pisces." Peter spread his legs invitingly. He lifted his arms, reaching for his shifter. "Take me. I'm yours."

With a groan, Pisces sank down on top of him, nestling between his thighs. He pressed his still-hard cock against Peter's, sending delicious tingles through Peter's groin. Bracketing Peter's head with his hands, Pisces latched onto Peter's lips, taking his mouth in a kiss that ravished and claimed.

Peter moaned and shuddered, more than on board for the ride.

Pisces felt out of control in the best way possible. His mate lay supple and welcoming beneath him. He felt Peter wrap his legs around his waist, clutching him close. His mate fed him moans of pleasure as he writhed against Pisces.

The sounds and sensations were quickly going to Pisces's head, and even though he'd just enjoyed one of the best fucking releases of his life, he remained hard and ready, needing inside his mate.

Lube.

With a moan, Pisces broke the kiss. He panted harshly as he cast his attention to the side of the towel. Spotting what he needed, Pisces grabbed the tube of slick and made quick work of dousing his cock.

Even as Pisces hissed at the chill, his prick twitching at the stimulation, he poured another healthy dollop onto his fingers. After closing and tossing it aside, he focused on Peter's face as he reached down and found his mate's hole with unerring accuracy. Pisces pressed a finger inside and groaned upon feeling his human's body easily give way, allowing him to sink into Peter's tight, squeezing heat.

Upon feeling the sensation, Pisces groaned deeply. He eased his finger out and pushed back in. When Peter canted his hips and moved into his touch, Pisces added a second finger, crooking his digits in search of that special nub.

When Peter groaned and shuddered beneath him, Pisces issued a feral growl, knowing he'd found it. He repeated his ministrations, speeding up his movements. As much as Pisces wanted to take his time with his mate, his need drove him forward almost blindly.

Pisces soon added a third finger, easing it in beside the first two. Seeing and feeling Peter's slight hitch beneath him, he dredged up a measure of self-control and paused. He twisted his fingers just a little, allowing him to slide over Peter's prostate again.

Peter instantly groaned, and after another few seconds, he relaxed beneath him.

Lowering his head, Pisces captured Peter's lips once more. Where before it had been all teeth, tongues, and need, that time, he managed to keep it relaxed and teasing. At the same time, Pisces continued stretching his mate, getting him good and ready.

Lifting his head a little, breaking the kiss, Pisces held Peter's gaze. "Ready, my mate?" His voice came out more ragged than he'd ever heard it, betraying his desires.

"Ready, Pisces," Peter responded, sounding just as rough. "I'm ready. Mate us."

Pisces wouldn't have been able to deny that request, even if he'd wanted to, which he didn't. After easing his fingers free of Peter's channel, he gripped his base and quickly lined up his cock. He touched his crown to his mate's opening, and even that little stimulation seemed to shoot straight up his cock.

With a groan, Pisces shuddered. Breathing deeply, he struggled to get himself under control. When Peter wrapped his legs back around Pisces's waist and pushed against him harder, he accepted it was a losing battle.

Pisces growled low in his throat as he pushed forward, popping his crown past Peter's guardian muscle. Instantly, he was surrounded in the tightest, hottest, most exquisite heat of his life. Gritting his teeth, Pisces began to push forward slowly, deeper and deeper, barely resisting his urge to slam home fast and hard.

"Yessss, Pisces," Peter snarled. "Fill me."

Feeling Peter dig his heels into Pisces's back, pushing back against him, Pisces whimpered his mate's name ... and drove forward. He froze, buried balls deep. A shudder worked through his frame as he kept still, doing his best to give Peter a chance to adjust.

Peter trembled beneath him, worrying Pisces. Then his mate whined, "Don't stop. Please, move."

Relief flooded Pisces that he hadn't hurt his mate. When he felt Peter clench around his embedded length, all self-control fled. Pisces drew his hips back before swiftly reversing direction and slamming home once more. The feel of Peter's hot, silky chute sent every thought out of his mind as he rutted over and over.

Fingernails dug into Pisces's shoulders, and he reveled in the knowledge that he would wear Peter's marks. His balls began to draw tight again, and he desperately tried to hold on. He adjusted his angle just a little, and Peter barked a bliss-filled cry as he jolted beneath him. In the next instant, Pisces felt the heat of Peter's cream between them as his mate's body clamped onto his shaft.

Unable to hold off, Pisces slammed as deeply as possible as his orgasm rolled through his shaking body. He poured spurt after spurt into his lover, marking him on the inside. His senses soared, and he cried Peter's name.

As Pisces came down from the endorphin ride, his instinct took over. He sank his teeth into the flesh where Peter's neck met his shoulder. Biting deep, Pisces reveled in the taste of the blood welling up from the wound. He drank greedily of his mate's exquisite-tasting life-blood, bonding them for eternity.

Pisces took several deep swallows before coming back to himself. Humming, he eased his teeth out of Peter's flesh. He lapped over the marks, sealing the wound, and a deep sense of satisfaction flooded Pisces upon seeing the mark left behind.

My claiming mark.

Pisces wasn't certain how long he stared at the beautiful scar before Peter's slightly slurred, mumbled voice broke through his fog.

"You look smug."

Chuckling softly, Pisces grinned into the face of his mate. He loved the sated expression he found there. Peter's eyes were heavy-lidded, his pupils were dilated, and his lips were kiss-ravaged, and Pisces had never thought he looked sexier.

"Hell, yeah, I'm smug," Pisces admitted, running a fingertip over his mark. "You're mine."

"I'm yours," Peter confirmed. He smiled softly as he rubbed his palms over Pisces's shoulders. "Sorry about the nail marks on your shoulders."

"Don't be," Pisces countered. With a waggle of his brows, he told him, "I hope to help you put them there often."

Peter barked a laugh. "I'm onboard with that."

With a wink, Pisces teased, "Then welcome aboard, captain."

His mate's laughter was music to Pisces's ears.

CHAPTER EIGHT

Peering around the back deck, Peter watched his friends interact with each other, Pisces, and Ryley. All his buddies were of a similar age as himself — twenty-eight, give or take — but they were welcoming and friendly with his coworker. It wasn't the first time they'd met the man, but the instances were definitely few and far between.

Peter decided he needed to change that. Especially since it seemed the man was going through some sort of mid-life crisis. So far, as he listened to his buddies, he was certain that Jake was giving Ryley the best advice. His dark-haired friend wrote paranormal romance for a living, so it made sense.

"Look, Ryley." Jake leaned forward with his elbows resting on his thighs. "It's not about whether you like dick or like tits. It's about the person attached to the appendages." His smile appeared understanding and warm. "Sure, you can be attracted to them, but you need to talk to them and find out if you have common interests." With a shrug, Jake added, "Everything else is dynamics."

"Okay, I get what you mean about needing to have things in common, regardless of sex," Ryley responded, nodding slowly. "But dynamics? I don't get it."

"Motion," Jake replied slowly. "What motions you use. The action taken in the circumstance." His cheeks actually turned a little pink as he cleared his throat. "Now, I don't know shit about pleasing a woman, but I figure it takes different motions to get her goin' than it does a man." After taking a swig of his beer, Jake finished with, "As you do things, you listen to their body language and learn what they like and don't like. Same with a guy."

Ryley actually nibbled his bottom lip, his expression turning pensive, as if he were trying to process what Jake meant.

Fortunately, Link jumped in before Peter had to. Their group's fourth childhood friend was also bisexual. Tapping his beer bottle against Ryley's, Link drew the other paramedic's attention.

"So you start slowly exploring your lady's body, and you discover she doesn't like her nipples pinched, so you don't do it, but she loves to have her tits massaged, so you do that instead." Link's redheaded features started to darken, betraying his slight embarrassment at stating something so bluntly. "Same with a guy," he continued gamely. "Some guys like their nipples pinched. Some like their ass squeezed. Some like their balls fondled, and others are too sensitive and it turns 'em off." Focusing on his beer bottle, Link finished, "It's about exploration. The journey, not necessarily the destination of getting off."

"Although getting off is nice," Colton stated with a chuckle.

"Colt," Waylon rumbled, tossing his beer bottle cap at his partner good-naturedly. "We're tryin' to help here."

Colton caught the cap with ease and tossed it aside. "Just sayin'," he countered, lifting his hands in placation. Then he sobered and focused on Ryley. "But the guys are right. If you're actually interested in a relationship with someone you're attracted to, male or female, you have to care about what pleases them, too, just as much as you have to find things in common."

"God, I feel like I've been such an asshole all my life," Ryley muttered, shaking his head. Before taking a deep swig of beer, he admitted, "The biggest complaint I get from women I've dated is that I don't listen, and I don't make time for them."

"Ryley," Pisces cut in. "If you were interested in making something work with any of those women, you would have made the time." He carried the burgers and brats to the grill he'd started before heading into the house. "That's the real difference. Whoever you're attracted to, you have to decide if you're invested enough to put them first sometimes." Then Pisces pointed his spatula at him. "But not all the time because then you're a doormat, and that ain't good for either one of you."

Ryley nodded, looking serious.

Trying to lighten the mood, Peter rose to his feet. "Hell, maybe you just need a different prospect pool." He crossed his deck and paused at his coworker's side. "We'll put our heads together and make a list of places you haven't been . . . or haven't been to in a few years." With a scoff, Peter added, "If you really want a relationship, anyway. If you just want to get your dick sucked, we can take you to a gay club." He watched the way Ryley's eyes widened as he smirked at him. "There are plenty of young twinks who'd be happy to drop to their knees for a muscular guy like you."

"Uh, thanks?" Ryley glanced around at the group, looking decidedly uncomfortable.

Peter chuckled again and started toward the house. "I'm gonna hit the head, then start bringin' out the fixin's for our burgers and brats." He paused at the grill beside where Pisces was placing everything on the racks. "How long?" Then Peter tipped his chin up in a silent request.

Pisces didn't disappoint. He immediately dipped his head and pecked a kiss to Peter's lips. As Pisces straightened, a warm smile curved his lips.

"Ten minutes," Pisces told him. "Maybe a bit longer."

Peter nodded. "Plenty of time."

"Want me to give you a hand?" Waylon offered, starting to

rise from his chair. "Slice a tomato or something?"

With a nod, Peter told him, "Grab the package of cheese slices from the fridge. Pisces will need them in a few. Everything else is prepped." Eyeing the outdoor coffee table, Peter added, "Maybe grab another couple of bags of chips, so no one has to wait for me."

"Will do."

Peter led the way inside with Waylon following him. As soon as the sliding door was closed, his buddy asked, "Things going well with Pisces?" He stared pointedly at Peter's shifter's mark on his shoulder. "I see he claimed you."

Smiling, happiness flooding him, Peter told him, "Yep. Things are going real well." Then he hurried down the hall toward the bathroom.

After Peter relieved himself and washed his hands, he opened the door and stepped back into the hall. A shadow to his right caught his attention, and he froze. From out of his front sitting room appeared a familiar disheveled appearance.

The rogue is in my house.

"How?" The word was out of Peter's mouth before he could think better of it.

The rogue's red-irised eyes fixated on him, and he curved his lips into a creepy smile. "Your shifter revealed my location to a coven." He sniffed the air exaggeratedly even as he eyed him with hunger in his eyes. "So I'm going to drain you dry, causing him to go insane." A crazy light filled his expression. "It'll be perfect vengeance before I have to move on."

"Oh, fuck," Peter whispered.

"No thanks," the rogue teased even as he started stalking toward Peter. "Not gay."

Peter spun and launched back into the bathroom. He had just enough time to slam the door in the rogue's face and lock the door before the crazy vampire's body slammed into it. The vibration caused Peter to tumble to the ground.

Shimmying sideways, Peter braced his back against the

wall and his feet against the bottom of the door before the door shook again. The wood around the lock began to crack. As Peter screamed Pisces's name, he would never be so grateful that his house wasn't a newer construction, and it still had thick, solid interior doors instead of the hollow-cored ones.

Pisces took the package of pre-sliced cheese from Waylon. "Thanks, Waylon."

After acknowledging Pisces's words, the large black male moved off to place the three bags of chips—one with corn tortillas, one barbeque-flavored, and a third plain for the dips on the table—Pisces opened the package. There were two types of cheese inside. He placed pepperjack cheese on half the burgers and medium cheddar on the rest.

No one had wanted just a plain burger. Pisces had asked.

Just as Pisces closed the lid, a trio of men appeared from several directions. Immediately, Colton leaped to his feet and ushered Waylon behind him. The seahorse shifter positioned himself between two of the strangers and his mate, as well as the other humans.

Pisces finally registered the scent of vampires, and he hurried to do the same.

The single vampire between himself and the group leveled a dark look upon Pisces. "Where is the rogue?" he demanded. "We know he's here." The vampire took a menacing step forward. "Are you hiding him?"

For an instant, Pisces remained tongue-tied.

"We're not hiding any rogues," Colton declared, yanking Pisces out of his confusion.

"You're from Master Aldor Bercham's coven," Pisces guessed, causing the speaker—who had to be the leader—to narrow his eyes suspiciously. "I'm Pisces," he continued gamely. "I'm the one who gave your coven his location. I'm—

"

The crash of something on wood was followed by Peter screaming Pisces's name.

"Shit. He's inside," Pisces barked.

Dismissing the strangers—they were obviously a hunting party from the coven—Pisces sprinted across the deck. His mate had been in the bathroom. He knew that room had a frosted glass window, so that was where he headed.

Pisces didn't bother opening it. Instead, he skidded to a stop and used an elbow to smash the glass. Spotting Peter on the floor, his feet braced against the door, Pisces leaped through the opening.

A second later, Pisces whipped his shirt over his head and wrapped the fabric around his hand and wrist. After using the wrapped appendage to clear away the glass, he tossed his ruined shirt to the floor. Pisces grabbed Peter under the arms and draped him over his shoulder.

As Pisces leaped out the broken window, taking his mate with him, he heard the door crash open behind him. He landed easily and rushed toward where Colton had herded his mate and the other humans. After setting Peter on the deck and handing him off to his friends' waiting arms, Pisces spun in preparation of squaring off against the rogue.

He didn't have to.

Even as the rogue landed from his own leap out the window, the pair of vampires Colton had been facing surrounded him. The rogue turned back as if ready to go back through the house. That was thwarted by the appearance of the vampire who'd been their speaker appearing in the window.

The pair slashed out with their claws—three-inch-long talons that extended from their fingers. One eviscerated the rogue across his belly. The second went for the rogue's throat. A second later, the speaker had jumped out the window and landed behind him.

The speaker grabbed the heavily bleeding rogue's shoulder and spun him around. He punched his taloned hand through the rogue's chest. After yanking out the male's bleeding heart, with a disdainful look, he allowed his dead body to fall to the deck planking.

Silence reigned, but only for an instant.

"What the fuck?" Ryley whispered, clearly shocked.

"Take a deep breath, man," Waylon encouraged, gripping the paramedic's shoulders. "You're okay."

Pisces wrapped his arms around Peter and clutched him to his chest. Rubbing up and down his trembling mate's back, he kissed his temple while whispering, "You're safe, my mate. You're safe."

For several long heartbeats, Peter continued to shiver against him. Finally, he let out a long breath and sagged against him. His arms came around Pisces, squeezing him back.

"I knew you'd come," Peter mumbled.

"I'll always come," Pisces declared, continuing to soothe his mate. Letting out a growl, he admitted, "Although, I hope you're never in that kind of situation again."

Peter let out a soft laugh that held no mirth. "Me, too."

"You said you're Pisces?"

Pisces turned his attention to the vampire who'd ripped out the rogue's heart, but he didn't let go of his mate. He couldn't. Not right then. Pisces needed to feel Peter in his arms to assure himself that his human was safe.

"I am," Pisces confirmed, ignoring the way the rogue was using a cloth to clean his talons. That didn't mean he allowed Peter to turn his head and look at the vampire just yet.

"You're the pod tracker, then." The vampire tucked the cloth into his back pocket before holding out his right hand. "I'm Enforcer Lawson."

After shifting Peter to be tucked against his side with his

left hand, Pisces reached out and took the vampire's hand. "Thank you," he decided to go with.

"It's my job," Lawson replied dismissively. His gaze strayed to Colton and the humans. "Need clean-up?"

"Just the body and my window," Peter responded with a scoff. "But I'll take care of the window if you deal with the body."

"Consider it done," Lawson told him, although his attention remained on those behind them. "But I meant the unbonded humans."

"Uh, no," Peter quickly countered. "My friends know about paranormals." He winced as he glanced behind them. "Well, at least, most of them."

Pisces squeezed Peter's side and whispered, "Maybe we should have Ryley wiped."

Peter nibbled his bottom lip, clearly uncertain as he looked to where a pale and wide-eyed Ryley was sitting.

"It won't take much," Lawson assured, a hint of a smile curving his lips. "It won't hurt him, and he'll never know."

Groaning, Peter shook his head even as he muttered, "Whatever your protocol is."

Lawson headed toward Ryley. Even though he moved slowly, he still caught the attention of the trembling older paramedic. The vampire's irises bled to red, and a second later, Ryley flinched. He lifted his hand to his head and groaned.

"Shit, what is that?" Ryley asked, a whine in his voice as he rubbed his temple.

"Huh." Lawson backed off, his blond brows lifting to his hairline. He turned his attention back to Pisces, his eyes once again blue. "You need to tell your alpha that he's immune."

"Immune?" Peter questioned first. "What's that mean?"

Lawson smirked as he rolled one wide shoulder in a half-shrug. "It means I can't trance him. From my experience, Fate's protecting him." His grin showcased his fangs. "I'd bet he has a paranormal mate out there somewhere, and Fate's prepping him."

"Really?" Pisces had never heard that before. Of course, the human was going through a change already, so who knew what Fate had in store for him? "Well, guess we'll take him back to *World of Aquatica*."

After a glance over his shoulder where his vampire buddies were removing all evidence of the rogue being there — other than glass — Lawson refocused on them. "Thanks for the tip, Pisces." He stuck out his hand again. "Good working with you."

"Uh, thanks." Pisces shook the vampire's hand again, and within the next few minutes, they were gone as was the body and the traces of blood.

"How the hell did they do that?" Link murmured, coming to stand beside them.

"Not a clue," Pisces admitted. He peered at Link just as the smell of burning meat perfumed the air. With a groan, Pisces asked, "Will you get the meat off the grill? See if anything is salvageable?"

"You can eat after that?" Link stared at him askance even as he moved toward the grill.

Colton shrugged. "You get used to it. Shit happens."

"So very true," Peter mused, shaking his head. Peering up at Pisces, he told him, "I know this sounds weird, but even after everything that's happened here, I don't want to move out of my house." As if worried that Pisces would object, Peter added, "It was my grandma's."

Pisces dipped his head and pecked a kiss to Peter's lips. "I already talked to Alpha Kaiser about me living here with you."

"You did?"

Loving the pleasure that filled Peter's beautiful features, Pisces nodded. "Yup. This is your home. And you're my home. That means it's my home, too."

"Thank you, Pisces," Peter whispered, standing on his toes and pressing their lips together.

Pisces was only too happy to kiss Peter right back. Commuting to work had never sounded so good when he knew he had his mate waiting for him at home.

About the Author

Charlie started writing fantasy when she was eight, and after stumbling onto her first erotic romance at age nineteen, she realized her true calling. She now focuses on writing gay erotic romance, normally of the paranormal variety, with heroes of all kinds. With the help and support of her husband, Charlie finally fulfilled one of her life-long goals . . . move to acreage with her horses. You can often find her curled up with her laptop and a cup of tea or glass of wine, creating her next adventure. Charlie enjoys exploring the mountains of her new Oregon home on horseback, 4-wheeler, or motorcycle.

She can be reached at ch.richards2010@yahoo.com

Or visit her at www.charlie-richards.com.

www.ingramcontent.com/pod-product-compliance
Lightning Source LLC
Chambersburg PA
CBHW071201130626
46555CB00004B/1535